was proudly printed and bound in the

U.S.A.

By the fine folks at Worzalla Publishing in Stevens Point, Wisconsin.
A special thanks to Worzalla for their kindness and support of this book.

Thank you to Marge Moriarity for her punctuality and her
chocolate chip cookies!

And Vivian Waxon Kaminski for her ongoing enthusiastic support.

Proofreading, Graphic Liaisons, LLC

Library of Congress Cataloging-in-Publication Data

Johnson, Judith C.
Poppel
Author, Judith Carol Johnson
Illustrator, Aaron Joel Moriarity

p.   cm.

SUMMARY: Poppel is a small boy who lives next to an enchanted forest with his
Great Aunt Flo. One day he wanders into the forest to see if he can befriend the
critters, only to find out that animals cannot become friends with people. Then
Oliver Owl discovers a way to befriend Poppel.

Copyright   ©2002 Judith C. Johnson

LCCN 2002093891

ISBN 0-9724193-0-6

[1. Friendship - Juvenile Fiction. 2. Enchanted Forest - Fiction. 3. Animals - Fiction.]
I. Title. II. Johnson, Judith C. III. Moriarity, Aaron Joel

[E]   813.6   dc21

First Edition   1 2 3 4 5 6 7 8 9 10

Look for other  books and toys.
www.poppelpress.com

Poppel Press
Publishing for the benefit of children

Poppel

Poppel's purpose,
is to bring Help, Happiness, and Hope
to all of the children at The Childrens' Hospitals,
all across America; by donating 50% of the profits of Poppel
books, toys, and merchandise to the Childrens' Hospitals.

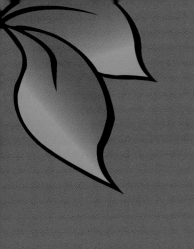

This book is dedicated to:
~ My children ~
My Angel Alayna Marie,
Who is my inspiration...
Justin, my son,
Who is my precious POPPEL...
And
Jacquelyn (Jacy),
My daughter,
Who keeps me smiling
With her "happy little people" ~

And a special thank you to my Illustrator,
Aaron Joel Moriarity, without whom
this book would not have been
so colorful, and so much fun.

Thanks,
Judy

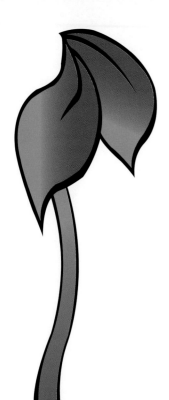

This book belongs to:

_____

Given by:

_____

Date:

_____

Once in a time,

Not so long ago . . .

Lived a boy

Named POPPEL

And his Great Aunt,

Flo . . .

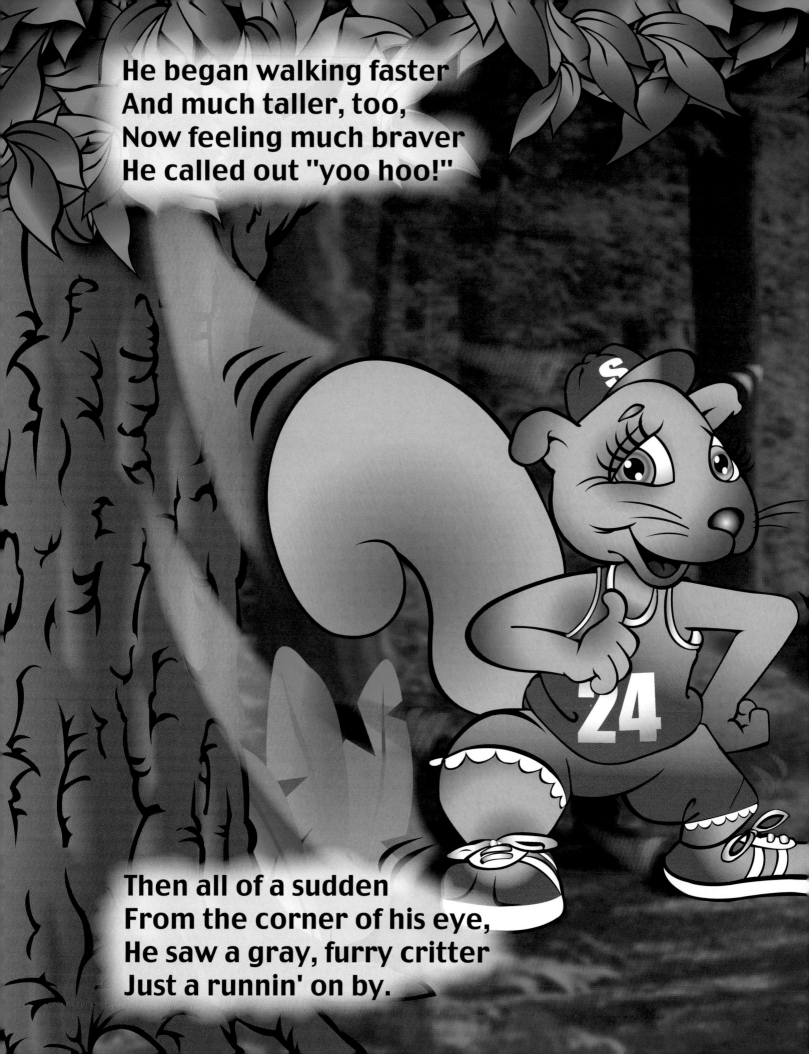

He began walking faster
And much taller, too,
Now feeling much braver
He called out "yoo hoo!"

Then all of a sudden
From the corner of his eye,
He saw a gray, furry critter
Just a runnin' on by.

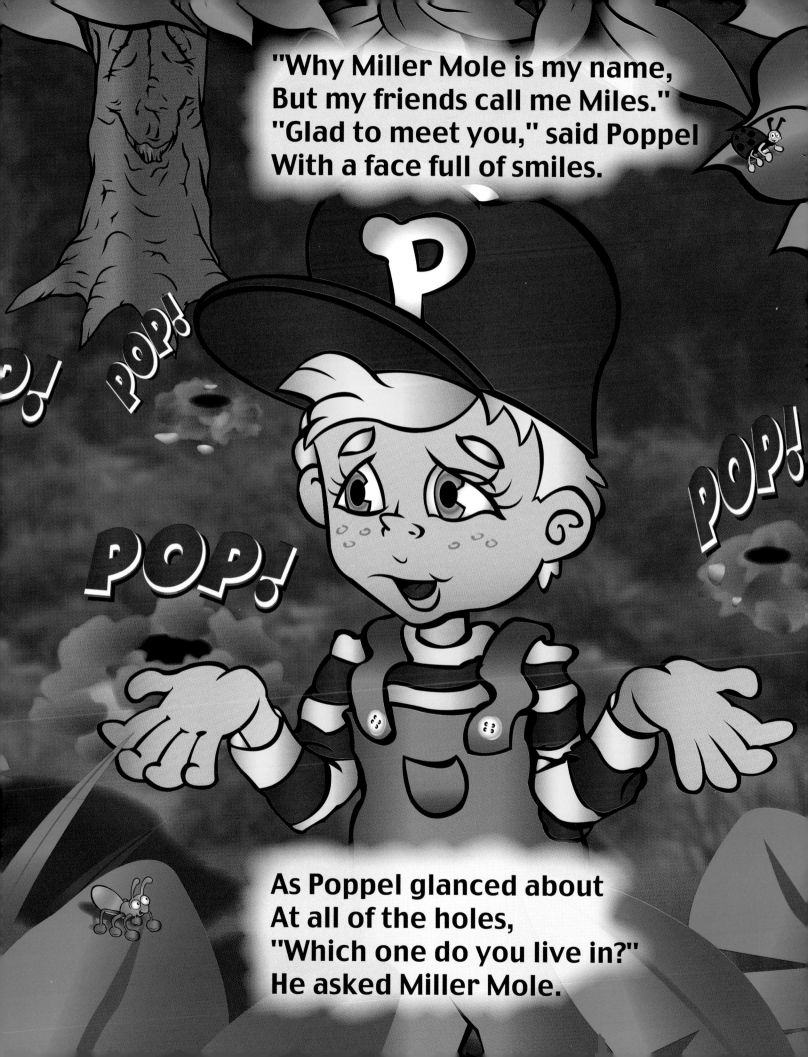

As Poppel walked on
letting out a big sigh,
I think you could spot
A tear in his eye.

Then Poppel looked up
In the sky so blue,
And thought he heard someone
Calling out "yoo- hoo!"

He flew round and round
Wondering what he could do...
Then flew back in the forest
To find his friends, too.

First Ollie found Fancy
In her hole in a tree.
He shouted, "Hey Fancy!
Come along with me!"

"We'll be your friends!"
They all shouted with glee!
And now POPPEL was happy,
As happy can be!!

The adventure begins......